SPONGEBOB DETECTIVE PANTS
THE CASE OF THE VANISHED SQUIRREL

by David Lewman
illustrated by Harry Moore

Based on the TV series *SpongeBob SquarePants*® created by Stephen Hillenburg as seen on Nickelodeon®

SIMON SPOTLIGHT/NICKELODEON

An imprint of Simon & Schuster Children's Publishing Division · New York London Toronto Sydney · 1230 Avenue of the Americas, New York, New York 10020
First Edition
2 4 6 8 10 9 7 5 3 1
ISBN-13: 978-1-4169-4939-8   ISBN-10: 1-4169-4939-9

It was a windy day in Bikini Bottom. SpongeBob was staring out the window. "Hey, Patrick, let's go see if Sandy wants to blow some bubbles with us and watch them blow away in the wind," SpongeBob suggested.

"Huh?" Patrick said, waking suddenly from his nap.

On Sandy's door there was a note. SpongeBob read the note aloud. "It says 'I've taken.'"
Patrick picked another page up off the ground. "This one just says 'Sandy.'"
SpongeBob's eyes widened. "'I've taken Sandy!'" he cried.
"Where did you take her?" Patrick asked.
"I didn't take her, Patrick. I think Sandy's been squirrel-napped by whoever wrote this note. Forget bubble-blowing, buddy, this is a case for SpongeBob DetectivePants!"
"And his faithful assistant, Patrick . . . uh . . . PatrickPants!" cried Patrick.

"Let's comb the ground for clues!" SpongeBob announced. He looked around and spotted an acorn cap on the ground. He held it up triumphantly. "Aha! Do you know what this is, Pat?"

Patrick squinted at the acorn cap. "A tiny hat?" he guessed.

"It's the top from one of those nuts Sandy eats. She must have dropped it when the squirrel-nappers took her! Look," he continued. "There's a trail! We have to follow it."

The trail led to Mussel Beach, where Larry the Lobster sat munching on acorns. "Where did you get those nuts, Larry?" SpongeBob asked suspiciously.

"Sandy gave 'em to me," Larry answered. "A few days ago, at her morning workout."

"You squirrel-napped her, didn't you?" Patrick blurted out.

"What are you talking about, dude?" Larry said, munching on the tasty nuts. "We worked out and then she left."

Then Patrick noticed something in the sand. "Look, Mr. DetectivePants, over there! What is it?"

"Hmm," said SpongeBob, studying it carefully. "It's an eye patch. The kind of eye patch worn by . . . PIRATES!"

Larry chuckled. "Yeah, I think there were some kids playing—"

"I've heard of pirates hanging around these parts," SpongeBob interrupted.

"You mean, like the Flying Dutchman?" asked Patrick.

"Exactly. He probably dropped this while taking Sandy to his ghostly ship!"

"How do we find his ghostly ship?"

"Isn't that it, right there?" Larry said, pointing.

SpongeBob and Patrick climbed a rope up to the Flying Dutchman's ship. They tiptoed across the deck, trying to be as quiet as possible, but suddenly the Flying Dutchman came zooming out at them!

"WHO DARES TO BOARD MY SHIP WITHOUT PERMISSION?" he roared.

"I d-d-dare," SpongeBob managed to squeak. "SpongeBob DetectivePants. I'm here to save Sandy."

The Flying Dutchman looked puzzled. "Who's Cindy?"

"Yeah, SpongeBob, who's Cindy?" Patrick asked, confused.

"Not Cindy, *Sandy*," SpongeBob said. "She's my friend, and she's a squirrel."

"There's no squirrel here," growled the old pirate. "Squirrels aren't allowed on my ship. AND NEITHER ARE YOU!"

With that, the Flying Dutchman tossed SpongeBob and Patrick overboard!

SpongeBob and Patrick landed on the ground with a THUD. They picked themselves up and brushed the sand off their clothes.

"If the Flying Dutchman didn't take Sandy, who did?" Patrick asked.

SpongeBob looked discouraged. "I don't know, Patrick. Maybe I'm not such a great detective after all."

"You're the best detective I've ever worked with," Patrick said loyally.

"Thanks, Pat," SpongeBob said.

Having no more clues to follow, the duo began to walk home.

When they got to Squidward's house, they heard a horrible noise!

"Pat, it sounds like someone yelping! Maybe it's Sandy!"

They burst through Squidward's front door.

"Don't you people knock?" Squidward grumbled. "I'm practicing my clarinet and it sounds . . ." Squidward got choked up. "Beautiful."

"You're under arrest, you clarinet player!" Patrick bellowed.

"Pat, Sandy's not yelping. That noise was Squidward's clarinet playing. Hey, Squidward, when was the last time you saw Sandy?"

"A few days ago. You weren't home so she came over to ask me to tell you to water her plants for her. I would have told you earlier, but I was avoiding you."

"Where was she going when she left?" SpongeBob asked eagerly.

"I think she said something about the bus station," Squidward answered. "Now, will you two get out of my house?"

"To the Bikini Bottom Bus Station!" announced SpongeBob.

At the bus station, SpongeBob and Patrick kept their eyes peeled for more clues. "See anything suspicious, Patrick?" SpongeBob asked.

"Nope," he answered. "Just Sandy."

"SANDY?!"

SpongeBob whirled around and saw Sandy getting off a bus.

"It sure was nice of you to meet me here!" Sandy said cheerfully.

"Sandy!" cried SpongeBob. "We thought you'd been squirrel-napped. What happened? We found these on your door. They say 'I've taken Sandy!'"

Sandy looked at the notes. "Aw, little buddy—I wrote this," she explained. "Hmm, the wind must've torn it up. The whole note said: 'I've taken a trip to Texas fer the annual Horn-Lockin' Competition. Back soon, Sandy.'"

Back at Sandy's treedome, the three friends celebrated her return.

"Thanks for trying to find me! That was real swell of y'all," Sandy said.

"You're welcome, Sandy," he answered. "I, SpongeBob DetectivePants, officially call this case closed!"

"How'd it end?" asked Patrick eagerly.

"It worked out perfectly!" replied SpongeBob, and everyone started to laugh.